HOCUS-FOCUS

HOCUS-FOCUS

THE FAMOUS PICTURE PUZZLES FROM THE SUNDAY COMIC SECTION

HAL KAUFMAN
BOB SCHROETER

TOR
A TOM DOHERTY ASSOCIATES BOOK

This is a work of fiction. All the characters and events portrayed in this book are fictional, and any resemblance to real people or incidents is purely coincidental.

HOCUS-FOCUS

A Tor Book

Published by Tom Doherty Associates, 8-10 W. 36th St., New York City, N. Y. 10018

First printing, December, 1983

ISBN: 0-812-57-025-1

Printed in the United States of America

Distributed by Pinnacle Books. 1430 Broadway, New York, N. Y. 10018

HOCUS-FOCUS

CAN YOU TRUST YOUR EYES? There are at least six differences in drawing details between top and bottom panels. How quickly can you find them? Check answers with those below.

Differences: 1. Surfboard is changed. 2. Hat is smaller. 3. Umbrella is different. 4. Surfer is repositioned. 5. Sailboat is different. 6. Bathing suit is changed.

HOCUS-FOCUS

CAN YOU TRUST YOUR EYES? There are at least six differences in drawing details between top and bottom panels. How quickly can you find them? Check answers with those below.

Differences: 1. Hat is smaller. 2. Purse strap is missing. 3. Man's coat is different. 4. Veil is shorter. 5. Hair is different. 6. Arm is repositioned.

HOCUS-FOCUS

CAN YOU TRUST YOUR EYES? There are at least six differences in drawing details between top and bottom panels. How quickly can you find them? Check answers with those below.

Differences: 1. Hat is changed. 2. Collar is smaller. 3. Handbag is repositioned. 4. Scarf is different. 5. Street lines are missing. 6. Wall is different.

HOCUS-FOCUS

CAN YOU TRUST YOUR EYES? There are at least six differences in drawing details between top and bottom panels. How quickly can you find them? Check answers with those below.

Differences: 1. Jacket is shorter. 2. Trap is larger. 3. Spare tire is missing. 4. Cart is missing. 5. Post is missing. 6. Chrome strip is missing.

CAN YOU TRUST YOUR EYES? There are at least six differences in drawing details between top and bottom panels. How quickly can you find them? Check answers with those below.

Differences: 1. Mane is different. 2. Haunch is missing. 3. Tail is missing. 4. Hat is different. 5. Buckle is different. 6. Bracelet is missing.

CAN YOU TRUST YOUR EYES? There are at least six differences in drawing details between top and bottom panels. How quickly can you find them? Check answers with those below.

Differences: 1. Bikini is different. 2. Manikin's neck is different. 3. Hair is different. 4. Sleeve is shorter. 5. Purse is missing. 6. Skirt is shorter.

HOCUS-FOCUS

CAN YOU TRUST YOUR EYES? There are at least six differences in drawing details between top and bottom panels. How quickly can you find them? Check answers with those below.

Differences: 1. Sailboat is missing. 2. Bird is missing. 3. Window is missing. 4. Sun is missing. 5. Bell post is lower. 6. Island is smaller.

HOCUS-FOCUS

CAN YOU TRUST YOUR EYES? There are at least six differences in drawing details between top and bottom panels. How quickly can you find them? Check answers with those below.

Differences: 1. Bottle is missing. 2. hat is different. 3. Handle is missing. 4. Tie is different. 5. Towel is different. 6. Oval pane in door is different.

HOCUS-FOCUS

CAN YOU TRUST YOUR EYES? There are at least six differences in drawing details between top and bottom panels. How quickly can you find them? Check answers with those below.

Differences: 1. Tail is missing. 2. Ear is different. 3. Feather is missing. 4. Pocketbook is different. 5. Jacket is different. 6. Bowl is empty.

CAN YOU TRUST YOUR EYES? There are at least six differences in drawing details between top and bottom panels. How quickly can you find them? Check answers with those below.

Differences: 1. Tree is different. 2. Belt is missing. 3. Number is missing. 4. Apron is different. 5. Towel bar is missing. 6. Collar is different.

HOCUS-FOCUS

CAN YOU TRUST YOUR EYES? There are at least six differences in drawing details between top and bottom panels: How quickly can you find them? Check answers with those below.

Differences: 1. Pennant is repositioned. 2. Sleeve is different. 3. Stocking is different. 4. Switch is missing. 5. Racket is missing. 6. Mirror is different.

HOCUS-FOCUS

CAN YOU TRUST YOUR EYES? There are at least six differences in drawing details between top and bottom panels. How quickly can you find them? Check answers with those below.

Differences: 1. Golf club is missing. 2. Strap is missing. 3. Bench is missing. 4. Bumper is missing. 5. Belt is missing. 6. Hat is different.

HOCUS-FOCUS

CAN YOU TRUST YOUR EYES? There are at least six differences in drawing details between top and bottom panels. How quickly can you find them? Check answers with those below.

Differences: 1. Picture is missing. 2. Sofa is different. 3. Tie is missing. 4. Belt is missing. 5. Boy's shirt is different. 6. Arm is repositioned.

CAN YOU TRUST YOUR EYES? There are at least six differences in drawing details between top and bottom panels. How quickly can you find them? Check answers with those below.

Differences: 1. Bird is missing. 2. Letter "S" is missing. 3. Bush is missing. 4. Window shade is missing. 5. Handle bar is missing. 6. Foot is repositioned.

HOCUS-FOCUS

CAN YOU TRUST YOUR EYES? There are at least six differences in drawing details between top and bottom panels. How quickly can you find them? Check answers with those below.

Differences: 1. Hairdo is different. 2. Hoe is different. 3. Sleeve is missing. 4. Drainpipe is missing. 5. Shovel handle is missing. 6. Foot is repositioned.

CAN YOU TRUST YOUR EYES? There are at least six differences in drawing details between top and bottom panels. How quickly can you find them? Check answers with those below.

Differences: 1. Sleeve is different. 2. Pocket is missing. 3. Panel opening is different. 4. Extended hand is different. 5. Phone is missing. 6. Sheet of paper is different.

HOCUS-FOCUS

CAN YOU TRUST YOUR EYES? There are at least six differences in drawing details between top and bottom panels. How quickly can you find them? Check answers with those below.

Differences: 1. Lampshade is different. 2. Switch is missing. 3. Pocket is missing. 4. Chair is different. 5. Sack is different. 6. Foot is repositioned.

HOCUS-FOCUS

CAN YOU TRUST YOUR EYES? There are at least six differences in drawing details between top and bottom panels. How quickly can you find them? Check answers with those below.

Differences: 1. Garbage can is missing. 2. Light is missing. 3. Whistle is missing. 4. Can is missing. 5. Bench support is different. 6. Bird is missing.

CAN YOU TRUST YOUR EYES? There are at least six differences in drawing details between top and bottom panels. How quickly can you find them? Check answers with those below.

Differences: 1. Hairdo is different. 2. Picture frame is different. 3. Apron is different. 4. Sofa is different. 5. Sleeve is different. 6. Locket is missing.

CAN YOU TRUST YOUR EYES? There are at least six differences in drawing details between top and bottom panels. How quickly can you find them? Check answers with those below.

Differences: 1. Locket is missing. 2. Sweater is different. 3. Handle is missing. 4. Pan is missing. 5. Sleeve is different. 6. Rug is different.

HOCUS-FOCUS

CAN YOU TRUST YOUR EYES? There are at least six differences in drawing details between top and bottom panels. How quickly can you find them? Check answers with those below.

Differences: 1. Flowers are missing. 2. Shade is different. 3. Chair cover is missing. 4. Hat is missing. 5. License plate is missing. 6. Glass is missing.

CAN YOU TRUST YOUR EYES? There are at least six differences in drawing details between top and bottom panels. How quickly can you find them? Check answers with those below.

Differences: 1. Street light is missing. 2. House number is missing. 3. Bus symbol is missing. 4. Skirt is different. 5. Sweater is different. 6. Poster (on pole) is different.

HOCUS-FOCUS

CAN YOU TRUST YOUR EYES? There are at least six differences in drawing details between top and bottom panels. How quickly can you find them? Check answers with those below.

Differences: 1. Squirrel is missing. 2. Woman is missing. 3. Hat is different. 4. Pocket is missing. 5. Pocketbook is different. 6. Gown is different.

HOCUS-FOCUS

CAN YOU TRUST YOUR EYES? There are at least six differences in drawing details between top and bottom panels. How quickly can you find them? Check answers with those below.

Differences: 1. Paper is missing. 2. Sweater neckline is different. 3. Glass is missing. 4. Fence is different. 5. Squirrel is missing. 6. Foot is repositioned.

HOCUS-FOCUS

CAN YOU TRUST YOUR EYES? There are at least six differences in drawing details between top and bottom panels. How quickly can you find them? Check answers with those below.

Differences: 1. Boat is missing. 2. Backrest is different. 3. Cloud is missing. 4. Footboard is missing. 5. Bathing suit different. 6. Swimmer missing.

CAN YOU TRUST YOUR EYES? There are at least six differences in drawing details between top and bottom panels. How quickly can you find them? Check answers with those below.

Differences: 1. Arm removed from fence. 2. Birdhouse missing. 3. Blind different. 4. Hose is different. 5. Apron different. 6. Frying pan is missing.

HOCUS-FOCUS

CAN YOU TRUST YOUR EYES? There are at least six differences in drawing details between top and bottom panels. How quickly can you find them? Check answers with those below.

Differences: 1. Motorcycle is missing. 2. House number is missing. 3. Refrigerator handle is missing. 4. Apron is different. 5. Sweater is different. 6. Drape is shorter.

HOCUS-FOCUS

CAN YOU TRUST YOUR EYES? There are at least six differences in drawing details between top and bottom panels. How quickly can you find them? Check answers with those below.

Differences: 1. Hamburger is missing. 2. Smoke is different. 3. Bird is missing. 4. Cap is missing. 5. Apron is shorter. 6. Spatula is replaced by fork.

HOCUS-FOCUS

CAN YOU TRUST YOUR EYES? There are at least six differences in drawing details between top and bottom panels. How quickly can you find them? Check answers with those below.

Differences: 1. Bedstead is different. 2. Dog's ear is different. 3. Hammer is reversed. 4. Board is shorter. 5. Sheet (on line) is shorter. 6. Doghouse door is different.

HOCUS-FOCUS

CAN YOU TRUST YOUR EYES? There are at least six differences in drawing details between top and bottom panels. How quickly can you find them? Check answers with those below.

Differences: 1. Parking meter is missing. 2. Mask is missing. 3. Home plate is different. 4. Bat is different. 5. Pitcher's leg is repositioned. 6. Fielder is repositioned.

HOCUS-FOCUS

CAN YOU TRUST YOUR EYES? There are at least six differences in drawing details between top and bottom panels. How quickly can you find them? Check answers with those below.

Differences: 1. Fireplug is missing. 2. Electric cord is different. 3 Lampshade is different. 4. Skirt is different. 5. Skate is missing. 6. Picture frame is added.

HOCUS-FOCUS

CAN YOU TRUST YOUR EYES? There are at least six differences in drawing details between top and bottom panels. How quickly can you find them? Check answers with those below.

Differences: 1. Antimacassar is missing. 2. Switch is missing. 3. Picture is missing. 4. End table is missing. 5. Earring is missing. 6. Book is missing.

HOCUS-FOCUS

CAN YOU TRUST YOUR EYES? There are at least six differences in drawing details between top and bottom panels. How quickly can you find them? Check answers with those below.

Differences: 1. Bar is lower. 2. Cap is missing. 3. Sign is missing. 4. Leg is repositioned. 5. Pencil is shorter. 6. Number is missing.

CAN YOU TRUST YOUR EYES? There are at least six differences in drawing details between top and bottom panels. How quickly can you find them? Check answers with those below.

Differences: 1—Candy dish is missing. 2. Hassock is missing. 3. Guitar is different. 4. Guitar string is missing. 5. Sleeve is missing. 6. Drape is shorter.

HOCUS-FOCUS

CAN YOU TRUST YOUR EYES? There are at least six differences in drawing details between top and bottom panels. How quickly can you find them? Check answers with those below.

Differences: 1. Light fixture is missing. 2. Refrigerator is different. 3. Apron is shorter. 4. Skirt is shorter. 5. Sweater neck is changed. 6. Hand is changed.

CAN YOU TRUST YOUR EYES? There are at least six differences in drawing details between top and bottom panels. How quickly can you find them? Check answers with those below.

Differences: 1. Scale is missing. 2. Bottle (on refrigerator) is missing. 3. Chair is lower. 4. Wrist watch is missing. 5. Handle is missing. 6. Bottle (on cabinet) is moved.

HOCUS-FOCUS

CAN YOU TRUST YOUR EYES? There are at least six differences in drawing details between top and bottom panels. How quickly can you find them? Check answers with those below.

Differences: 1. Collar is missing. 2. Jacket is different. 3. Light is missing. 4. Can is missing. 5. Arm is repositioned. 6. Belt is missing.

HOCUS-FOCUS

CAN YOU TRUST YOUR EYES? There are at least six differences in drawing details between top and bottom panels. How quickly can you find them? Check answers with those below.

Differences: 1. Bow is different. 2. Parking meter is missing. 3. Pocketbook missing. 4. Cake is missing. 5. Cake stand different. 6. Arm is repositioned.

CAN YOU TRUST YOUR EYES? There are at least six differences in drawing details between top and bottom panels. How quickly can you find them? Check answers with those below.

Differences: 1. Net is different. 2. Fireplug is missing. 3. Foot is repositioned. 4. Dog's ear is different. 5. Number is missing. 6. Wheel is missing.

CAN YOU TRUST YOUR EYES? There are at least six differences in drawing details between top and bottom panels. How quickly can you find them? Check answers with those below.

Differences: 1. Cone is different. 2. Light pole is missing. 3. Ice cream machine is missing. 4. Garbage can is missing. 5. Man's hand is missing. 6. Woman is missing.

CAN YOU TRUST YOUR EYES? There are at least six differences in drawing details between top and bottom panels. How quickly can you find them? Check answers with those below.

Differences: 1. Fire plug is missing. 2. License plate is missing. 3. Sidewalk is smaller. 4. Hand is changed. 5. Collar is changed. 6. Tree protector is shorter.

HOCUS-FOCUS

CAN YOU TRUST YOUR EYES? There are at least six differences in drawing details between top and bottom panels. How quickly can you find them? Check answers with those below.

Differences: 1. Puck is missing. 2. Stick is missing. 3. Portion of stick is repositioned. 4. Leg is repositioned. 5. Hair is different. 6. Double line is missing.

HOCUS-FOCUS

CAN YOU TRUST YOUR EYES? There are at least six differences in drawing details between top and bottom panels. How quickly can you find them? Check answers with those below.

Differences: 1. Bottle is missing. 2. Drawer is missing. 3. Block is missing. 4. Hairdo is different. 5. Sleeve is shortened. 6. Gun is repositioned.

HOCUS-FOCUS

CAN YOU TRUST YOUR EYES? There are at least six differences in drawing details between top and bottom panels. How quickly can you find them? Check answers with those below.

Differences: 1. Bush is missing. 2. Mane is different. 3. Rein loop is re-positioned. 4. Letter is missing. 5. Belt is missing. 6. Tail is different.

HOCUS-FOCUS

CAN YOU TRUST YOUR EYES? There are at least six differences in drawing details between top and bottom panels. How quickly can you find them? Check answers with those below.

Differences: 1. Bird is missing. 2. Heart is missing. 3. Swing board is different. 4. Rope end is missing. 5. Cap is different. 6. Hair is different.

HOCUS-FOCUS

CAN YOU TRUST YOUR EYES? There are at least six differences in drawing details between top and bottom panels. How quickly can you find them? Check answers with those below.

Differences: 1. Cat is missing. 2. Sofa is different. 3. Skirt is different. Switch is missing. 5. Antenna is different. 6. Foot is repositioned.

HOCUS-FOCUS

CAN YOU TRUST YOUR EYES? There are at least six differences in drawing details between top and bottom panels. How quickly can you find them? Check answers with those below.

Differences: 1. Pony tail is missing. 2. TV controls repositioned. 3. Pants leg is different. 4. Towel bar is missing. 5. Belt is missing. 6. Dishtowel is different.

HOCUS-FOCUS

CAN YOU TRUST YOUR EYES? There are at least six differences in drawing details between top and bottom panels. How quickly can you find them? Check answers with those below.

Differences: 1. Can is missing. 2. Sign is missing. 3. License plate is missing. 4. Car is missing. 5. Chimney is different. 6. Scarf is different.

HOCUS-FOCUS

CAN YOU TRUST YOUR EYES? There are at least six differences in drawing details between top and bottom panels. How quickly can you find them? Check answers with those below.

Differences: 1. Skirt is different. 2. Ashtray is missing. 3. Light fixture is different. 4. Clock is missing. 5. Hair is different. 6. Hand is repositioned.

CAN YOU TRUST YOUR EYES? There are at least six differences in drawing details between top and bottom panels. How quickly can you find them? Check answers with those below.

Differences: 1. Hair is different. 2. Picture is smaller. 3. Phone cord is different. 4. Drawer is missing. 5. Coat is shorter. 6. Heart is different.

CAN YOU TRUST YOUR EYES? There are at least six differences in drawing details between top and bottom panels. How quickly can you find them? Check answers with those below.

Differences: 1. Soap holder is missing. 2. Washcloth is missing. 3. Collar is different. 4. Apron is shorter. 5. Duck is missing. 6. Water level is lower.

HOCUS-FOCUS

CAN YOU TRUST YOUR EYES? There are at least six differences in drawing details between top and bottom panels. How quickly can you find them? Check answers with those below.

Differences: 1. Hat is different. 2. Sleeve is shorter. 3. Arm is repositioned. 4. Foot is repositioned. 5. Light switch is missing. 6. Lamp is different.

CAN YOU TRUST YOUR EYES? There are at least six differences in drawing details between top and bottom panels. How quickly can you find them? Check answers with those below.

Differences: 1. Light is different. 2. Cap is missing. 3. Cord is different. 4. Board is missing. 5. Belt is missing. 6. Cuff is missing.

HOCUS-FOCUS

CAN YOU TRUST YOUR EYES? There are at least six differences in drawing details between top and bottom panels. How quickly can you find them? Check answers with those below.

Differences: 1. Cap is smaller. 2. Hand is changed. 3. Pocket is missing. 4. Paper is missing. 3. Sofa is lower. 6. Skirt is shorter.

CAN YOU TRUST YOUR EYES? There are at least six differences in drawing details between top and bottom panels. How quickly can you find them? Check answers with those below.

Differences: 1. Apron is different. 2. Birdhouse is smaller. 3. Pencil is missing. 4. Tool board is different. 5. Vise handle is repositioned. 6. Board is shorter.

HOCUS-FOCUS

CAN YOU TRUST YOUR EYES? There are at least six differences in drawing details between top and bottom panels. How quickly can you find them? Check answers with those below.

Differences: 1. Lamp is missing. 2. Shovel is missing. 3. Mailbox is missing. 4. Briefcase is different. 5. Package is missing. 6. Collar is different.

CAN YOU TRUST YOUR EYES? There are at least six differences in drawing details between top and bottom panels. How quickly can you find them? Check answers with those below.

Differences: 1. Bat is missing. 2. Window is missing. 3. Glass is different. 4. Flower is missing. 5. Belt is missing. 6. Hat is repositioned.

CAN YOU TRUST YOUR EYES? There are at least six differences in drawing details between top and bottom panels. How quickly can you find them? Check answers with those below.

Differences: 1. Santa is missing. 2. Holly is missing. 3. Boy is missing. 4. Package is missing. 5. Purse is different. 6. Neckline is different.

HOCUS-FOCUS

CAN YOU TRUST YOUR EYES? There are at least six differences in drawing details between top and bottom panels. How quickly can you find them? Check answers with those below.

Differences: 1. Garage window is smaller. 2. Light fixture is missing. 3. Cat is missing. 4. Wreath is missing. 5. Tree is different. 6. Snow pile is lower.

CAN YOU TRUST YOUR EYES? There are at least six differences in drawing details between top and bottom panels. How quickly can you find them? Check answers with those below.

Differences: 1. Cat is missing. 2. Bottle is missing. 3. Pot handle is missing. 4. Neckline is different. 5. Cap is different. 6. Antenna is missing.

HOCUS-FOCUS

CAN YOU TRUST **your eyes? There are six differences in details between the top and bottom panels above. How quickly can you point out what these differences are? Answers below.**

Differences: 1. Cloud is reduced. 2. Mountain is smaller. 3. Clothespin is missing. 4. Shorts (on line) are smaller. 5. Foot is repositioned. 6. Hat is different.

HOCUS-FOCUS

CAN YOU TRUST YOUR EYES? There are at least six differences in drawing details between top and bottom panels. How quickly can you find them? Check answers with those below.

Differences: 1. Sweater is different. 2. Switch is missing. 3. Wastebasket is missing. 4. Pendant is missing. 5. Lamp is different. 6. Telephone wire is missing.

HOCUS-FOCUS

CAN YOU TRUST your eyes? There are six differences in details between the top and bottom panels above. How quickly can you point out what these differences are? Answers below.

Differences: 1. Boy's hat is missing. 2. Skirt is shortened. 3. Hand is repositioned. 4. Arm is repositioned. 5. Dog's collar is missing. 6. Dog's ear is shorter.

HOCUS-FOCUS

CAN YOU TRUST YOUR EYES? There are at least six differences in drawing details between top and bottom panels. How quickly can you find them? Check answers with those below.

Differences: 1. Glass is missing. 2. Hat is different. 3. Neckline is different. 4. Ladle is repositioned. 5. Pirate's sash is different. 6. Pirate's coat is shorter.

HOCUS-FOCUS

CAN YOU TRUST YOUR EYES? There are at least six differences in drawing details between top and bottom panels. How quickly can you find them? Check answers with those below.

Differences: 1. Player is missing. 2. Bench is missing. 3. Letter is missing. 4. Catcher's sleeve is different. 5. Hair is different. 6. Bat is repositioned.

HOCUS-FOCUS

CAN YOU TRUST YOUR EYES? There are at least six differences in drawing details between top and bottom panels. How quickly can you find them? Check answers with those below.

Differences: 1. Cloud is missing. 2. Star is missing. 3. Moon is missing. 4. Bush is missing. 5. Paddle is different. 6. Canoe is shorter.

HOCUS-FOCUS

CAN YOU TRUST YOUR EYES? There are at least six differences in drawing details between panels above. How quickly can you point out what these differences are? Answers below.

Differences: 1. Dog is missing. 2. Spare tire is repositioned. 3. Snowman is different. 4. Car door is missing. 5. Plant is missing. 6. Path is different.

HOCUS-FOCUS

CAN YOU TRUST YOUR EYES? There are at least six differences in drawing details between panels above. How quickly can you point out what these differences are? Answers below.

Differences: 1. Pocketbook is smaller. 2. Slingshot is missing. 3. Wagon handle is missing. 4. Small girl is repositioned. 5. Piece of wood is repositioned. 6. Roof is different.

HOCUS-FOCUS

CAN YOU TRUST YOUR EYES? There are at least six differences in drawing details between panels above. How quickly can you point out what these differences are? Answers below.

Differences: 1. Hat is different. 2. Jar is missing. 3. Watch is missing. 4. Rattle is missing. 5. Bib is different. 6. Apron is different.

HOCUS-FOCUS

CAN YOU TRUST YOUR EYES? There are six differences in drawing details between top and bottom panels. How quickly can you point out what these differences are? Answers below.

Differences: 1. Letter is missing. 2. Foot is repositioned. 3. Neckline is different. 4. Lamp base is different. 5. Sofa leg is missing. 6. Guitar is repositioned.

CAN YOU TRUST your eyes? There are six differences in details between the top and bottom panels above. How quickly can you point out what these differences are? Answers below.

Differences: 1. Scaffold is shorter. 2. Lid is missing. 3. Stirrer is missing. 4. Sleeve is different. 5. Brush is smaller. 6. Hand is missing.

HOCUS-FOCUS

CAN YOU TRUST YOUR EYES? There are six differences in drawing details between top and bottom panels. How quickly can you point out what the differences are? Answers below.

Differences: 1. Trowel is missing. 2. Puddle is missing. 3. Diving board support is missing. 4. Bathing cap is different. 5. Belt is removed. 6. Louver is missing.

HOCUS-FOCUS

CAN YOU TRUST YOUR EYES? There are six differences in drawing details between top and bottom panels. How quickly can you point out what these differences are? Answers below.

Differences: 1. Sweater is shorter. 2. Doorknob is missing. 3. Bow is missing. 4. Ashtray is missing. 5. Lampshade design is missing. 6. Bouquet is repositioned.

HOCUS-FOCUS

CAN YOU TRUST YOUR EYES? There are at least six differences in drawing details between top and bottom panels. How quickly can you find them? Check answers with those below.

Differences: 1. Hair is different. 2. Book is missing. 3. Man is missing. 4. Bead chain is missing. 5. Phone cord is missing. 6. Pocket is missing.

HOCUS-FOCUS

CAN YOU TRUST YOUR EYES? There are at least six differences in drawing details between top and bottom panels. How quickly can you find them? Check answers with those below.

Differences: 1. Christmas wreath is missing. 2. Rake is missing. 3. Snow bank is different. 4. Shovel handle is missing. 5. Woman's jacket is shorter. 6. Man's scarf is different.

HOCUS-FOCUS

CAN YOU TRUST YOUR EYES? There are at least six differences in drawing details between top and bottom panels. How quickly can you find them? Check answers with those below.

Differences: 1. Wastebasket is missing. 2. Foot is repositioned. 3. Clip is missing from clipboard. 4. Phone cord is different. 5. Hair is different. 6. Arm is repositioned.

HOCUS-FOCUS

CAN YOU TRUST YOUR EYES? There are at least six differences in drawing details between top and bottom panels. How quickly can you find them? Check answers with those below.

Differences: 1. Pocketbook is missing. 2. Hat is different. 3. Stethoscope is missing. 4. Sleeve is different. 5. Bugle is missing. 6. Second pillow is missing.

HOCUS-FOCUS

CAN YOU TRUST YOUR EYES? There are at least six differences in drawing details between top and bottom panels. How quickly can you find them? Check answers with those below.

Differences: 1. Number is different. 2. Straw container is repositioned. 3. Hairdo is different. 4. Hand is repositioned. 5. Spoon is missing. 6. Apron is different.

HOCUS-FOCUS

CAN YOU TRUST YOUR EYES? There are at least six differences in drawing details between top and bottom panels. How quickly can you point out these differences? Answers below.

Differences: 1. Pipe is missing. 2. Light is repositioned. 3. Wrench is reversed 4. Jug is missing. 5. Neckline is different. 6. Foot is repositioned.

HOCUS-FOCUS

CAN YOU TRUST YOUR EYES? There are at least six differences in drawing details between top and bottom panels. How quickly can you find them? Check answers with those below.

Differences: 1. Arm is moved. 2. Drape is shortened. 3. Lampshade is different. 4. Sleeve is shortened. 5. Eyeglasses are missing. 6. Foot is different.

HOCUS-FOCUS

CAN YOU TRUST YOUR EYES? There are at least six differences in drawing details between top and bottom panels. How quickly can you point out these differences? Answers below.

Differences: 1. Bird is missing. 2. Antimacassar is missing. 3. Lampshade is different. 4. Hat is different. 5. Pocketbook is missing. 6. Octopus' arm is missing.

HOCUS-FOCUS

CAN YOU TRUST YOUR EYES? There are six differences in drawing details between top and bottom panels. How quickly can you point out what these differences are? Answers below.

Differences: 1. Neckline is different. 2. Lampshade is different. 3. Book is missing. 4. Doily is missing. 5. Part of tie is missing. 6. Hairdo is different.

HOCUS-FOCUS

CAN YOU TRUST YOUR EYES? There are six differences in drawing details between top and bottom panels. How quickly can you point out what these differences are? Answers below.

Differences: 1. Vase is missing. 2. Pedal is missing. 3. Skate strap is missing. 4. Tree limb is missing. 5. Skirt is shorter. 6. Foot is repositioned.

HOCUS-FOCUS

CAN YOU TRUST YOUR EYES? **There are six differences in drawing details between top and bottom panels. How quickly can you point out what these differences are? Answer below.**

Differences: 1. Bird is missing. 2. Sleeve is shortened. 3. Golf club is shortened. 4. Man's pocket is missing. 5. Compartment is missing from golf bag. 6. Pail handle is missing.

HOCUS-FOCUS

CAN YOU TRUST your eyes? There are six differences in details between the top and bottom panels above. How quickly can you point out what these differences are? Answers below.

Differences: Bow is different. 2. Carpenter's rule is different. 3. Pocket is missing. 4. Neckline is different. 5. Sleeve is different. 6. Pencil is missing.

HOCUS-FOCUS

CAN YOU TRUST YOUR EYES? There are at least six differences in drawing details between top and bottom panels. How quickly can you find them? Check answers with those below.

Differences: 1. Man's hair is different. 2. Bird is missing. 3. Man with field glasses is missing. 4. Chimney is missing. 5. Neck chain is shortened. 6. Neckline is missing.

HOCUS-FOCUS

CAN YOU TRUST YOUR EYES? There are at least six differences in drawing details between top and bottom panels. How quickly can you find them? Check answers with those below.

Differences: 1. Lamp is missing. 2. Extension cord is missing. 3. Picture is missing. 4. Coffee spout is missing. 5. Foot is repositioned. 6. Skirt is shorter.